BECAUSE I'M YOUR DAD

WRITTEN by
AHMET ZAPPA

ILLUSTRATED by
DAN SANTAT

Disney • HYPERION BOOKS
NEW YORK

First Edition
10 9 8 7 6 5 4 3 2 1
G615-7693-2-13039
Printed in China

The illustrations were created using Adobe Photoshop. The text is set in 20-point Calibri Bold.

Library of Congress Cataloging-in-Publication Data
Zappa, Ahmet. • Because I'm your dad / [text, Ahmet Zappa ; illustrations, Dan Santat].—1st ed.
p. cm. • Summary: The son of an unconventional father promises a similar childhood for his newborn.
ISBN 978-1-4231-4774-9 • [1. Fathers—Fiction. 2. Father and child—Fiction.] I. Santat, Dan, ill. II. Title. III. Title:
Because I am your dad. • PZ7.Z258Be 2013 • [Fic]—dc23 • 2012002794

Visit www.disneyhyperionbooks.com

FOR MY LITTLE MONSTER

—A.E.R.Z.

. . . you're gonna get tickled.

Because I'm your dad, you might have an unusual first name.

Because I'm your dad, you can have spaghetti for breakfast,

French toast for dinner,
and rocky road ice cream in the bathtub.

Because I'm your dad, you'll grow up knowing robots are cool,

but monsters are even cooler.

Because I'm your dad, I'll always play rock music for you. **LOUD**.

And because I'm your dad, I'll buy you your very own drum set to rock out on.

Because I'm your dad, I'll make sure you know how to pogo-stick, and we'll make mud forts in the backyard.

I'll go to all your soccer games, even when they're far away.

And when you fall asleep
in the backseat,
I'll carry you inside.

Because I'm your dad, I'm going to teach you how to burp like a champion.

And I'll make sure your Halloween costume is always awesome.

Because I'm your dad, you might miss a few days of school

when I take you to
New York for a hot dog . . .

. . . or to Australia to see a platypus.

Because I'm your dad, I will miss you so much when I'm away,

ARRIVALS

and I promise to bring you back big surprises.

Because I'm your dad, I will always find you.

Because I'm your dad, you can sometimes stay up late with me to watch TV.

And I'll roll you up in a blanket like you're a burrito.

(I may also nibble on your toes, because they're so cute.)

Because I'm your dad, I will make up
funny stories for you at bedtime.

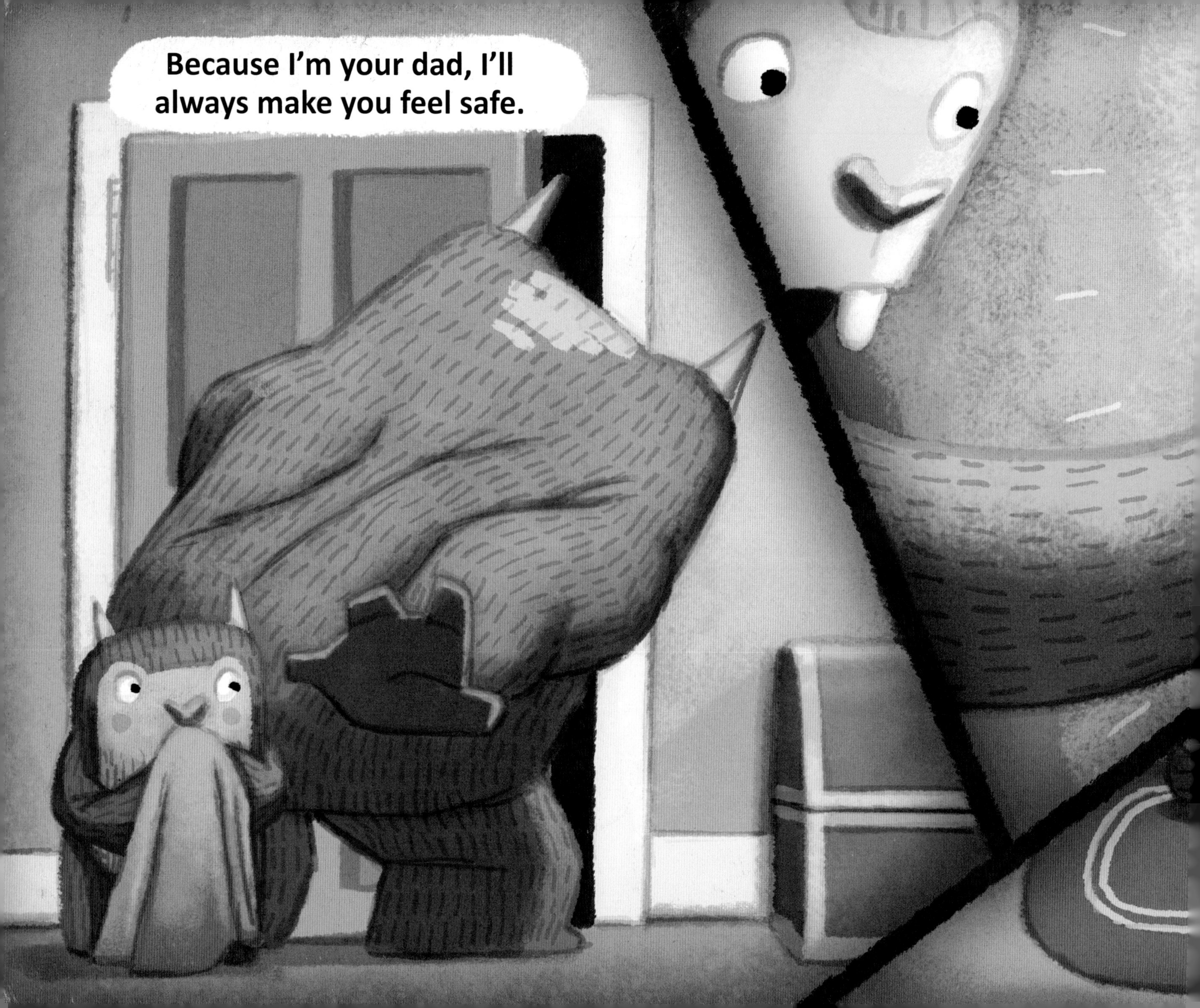
Because I'm your dad, I'll always make you feel safe.

I'm your dad, and I will do all these things for you and more . . .

. . . because that's what my dad did for me.